THE GHOSTS GO HAUNTING

HELEN KETTEMAN

PICTURES BY
ADAM RECORD

www.av2books.com

Your AV² Media Enhanced book gives you a fiction readalong online. Log on to www.av2books.com and enter the unique book code from this page to use your readalong.

AV² Readalong Navigation

HIGHLIGHTED TEXT

HOME 🏠

CLOSE ⊗

START READING

READ

> All children like to play.
> They dig in the dirt,
> they splash in water.
> They build roads and bridges
> for their cars and trucks.
> They play games
> like hide-and-go-seek.
> Children love to just run.
> What do you like to play?

20   21

AV² READALONG   BACK READ NEXT   INFO

TITLE INFORMATION

INFO

PAGE TURNING

BACK NEXT

PAGE PREVIEW

Go to **www.av2books.com**, and enter this book's unique code.

BOOK CODE

Q 3 6 4 8 5 6

AV² by Weigl brings you media enhanced books that support active learning.

First Published by

ALBERT WHITMAN & COMPANY
Publishing children's books since 1919

Published by AV² by Weigl
350 5ᵗʰ Avenue, 59ᵗʰ Floor New York, NY 10118
Websites: www.av2books.com   www.weigl.com

Library of Congress Control Number: 2015932707

ISBN 978-1-4896-3879-3 (hardcover)
ISBN 978-1-4896-3880-9 (single user eBook)
ISBN 978-1-4896-3881-6 (multi-user eBook)

Printed in the United States of America in Brainerd, Minnesota
2 3 4 5 6 7 8 9 0 19 18 17 16 15
112015
031115

Text copyright ©2014 by Helen Ketteman.
Illustrations copyright ©2014 by Albert Whitman & Company.
Published in 2014 by Albert Whitman & Company.

For Chrissy with love—HK

For my two (and one on the way)
adorable kids—AR

The ghosts go haunting one by one.
Boo! Boo!

The ghosts go haunting one by one.
Boo! Boo!

M.T. TOMBS
ELEMENTARY

4

The ghosts go haunting one by one.
The principal leaps from his chair and runs,
and they all go screeching
all over the school
for some Hal-lo-ween fun.

Boo!
Boo!
Boo!
Boo!
Boo!
Boo! Boo! Boo! Boo!

The witches go flying two by two.

Zoom! Zoom!

The witches go flying two by two.

Zoom! Zoom!

The witches go flying two by two.

They ZAP! their milk into witches' brew,

and they all go flying

all over the school

for some Hal-lo-ween fun.

The goblins go groaning three by three.

WOE! WOE!

The goblins go groaning three by three.

WOE! WOE!

The goblins go groaning three by three.
They chase the librarian up a tree,
and they all go groaning
all over the school
for some Hal-lo-ween fun.

WOE! WOE! WOE! WOE!

WOE! WOE!

WOE!

WOE!

The bats go diving four by four.
Flap! Flap!

The bats go diving four by four.
Flap! Flap!

12

The bats go diving four by four.
They chase the teachers out the front door,
and they all go diving
all over the school
for some Hal-lo-ween fun.

Flap! Flap!
Flap! Flap!
Flap! Flap!
Flap! Flap!

The monsters go stomping five by five.

CLOMP! CLOMP!

The monsters go stomping five by five.

CLOMP! CLOMP!

The monsters go stomping five by five.
They catch the computer repairman alive,
and they take him stomping
all over the school
for some Hal-lo-ween fun.

CLOMP!
CLOMP!
CLOMP!
CLOMP!

15

Black cats go hissing six by six.

Hiss! Hiss!

Black cats go hissing six by six.

Hiss! Hiss!

Black cats go hissing six by six.
The school nurse faints like a ton of bricks,
and they all go hissing
all over the school
for some Hal-lo-ween fun.

Hiss!

Hiss!

Hiss!

Hiss!

19

The spiders go creeping seven by seven.

Creep! Creep!

The spiders go creeping seven by seven.

Creep! Creep!

20

The spiders go creeping seven by seven.
The lunch ladies run and shout "Good heavens!"
and they all go creeping
all over the school
for some Hal-lo-ween fun.

Creep! Creep!
Creep! P.!
Creep!

Creep! Creep!
Creep! Creep!

The mummies go fright'ning eight by eight.
MOAN! MOAN!
The mummies go fright'ning eight by eight.
MOAN! MOAN!

The mummies go fright'ning eight by eight.
They scare the janitor stiff and straight,
and they all go fright'ning
all over the school
for some Hal-lo-ween fun.

MOAN! MOAN!
MOAN! MOAN!
MOAN! MOAN!
MOAN! MOAN!

The skeletons go rattling nine by nine. Clank! Clank!

The skeletons go rattling nine by nine. Clank! Clank!

The skeletons go rattling nine by nine.
The bus driver jumps off the bus to hide,
and they all go rattling
right past the bus
for some Hal-lo-ween fun.

Clank!
Clank!
Clank!
Clank!

clank!
clank!
clank!
clank!

The zombies go stumbling ten by ten.
Brains! Brains!

The zombies go stumbling ten by ten.
Brains! Brains!

The zombies go stumbling
ten by ten.
The coach begs for mercy
and then...
and then...

The whole school parties
the rest of the day
for some Hal-lo-ween fun!

HAPPY HALLO

Yay!Yay!Yay!Yay! Yay!Yay!Yay!Yay!

The creatures go marching...

1 X 1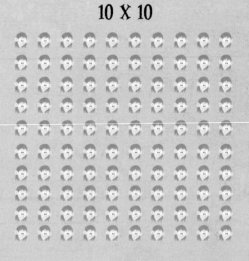

2 X 2

3 X 3
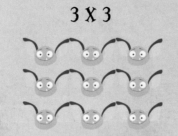

4 X 4

5 X 5

6 X 6

7 X 7

8 X 8

9 X 9

10 X 10